Do-wrong Ron

First published in 2003

Allen & Unwin
83 Alexander St
Crows Nest NSW 2065
Australia
Phone: (61 2) 8425 0100
Fax: (61 2) 9906 2218
Email: info@allenandunwin.com
Web: www.allenandunwin.com

National Library of Australia
Cataloguing-in-Publication entry:

Herrick, Steven.
Do-wrong Ron

ISBN 1 86508 661 4

1. Right and wrong—Juvenile fiction.
2. Grandmothers—Juvenile fiction. I. Magerl, Caroline. II. Title.

A823.3

Cover and text illustrations by Caroline Magerl
Cover and text design by Sandra Nobes
Typeset by Tou-Can Design
Printed in Australia by McPherson's Printing Group

1 3 5 7 9 10 8 6 4 2

Do-wrong Ron

Steven Herrick

pictures by
Caroline Magerl

ALLEN&UNWIN

Ron

My name is Ron.
Ron Holman.
Or *Do-wrong Ron*,
because I have this habit:
I do the wrong thing at the wrong time.
Or the right thing at the wrong time?
Or the wrong thing at the right time?

My best friend is my bedroom.
Me and my desk.
Me and my bed.
Me and my clothes all shoved in the wrong drawers.
Me and my soccer figures,
lying on their sides
as if they've just played a really hard game –
which reminds me of last season.
Oh dear.

Oh dear

1-1
with two minutes to go.
The coach calls,
'Ron, warm up.'
I can see it now.
The winning goal in the last second.
The coach says,
'Just kick the ball when it comes to you,
hard as you can.'
Simple.
The ball comes to me
as soon as I run onto the field,
so I kick it.
It's a stunning kick.
It goes thirty, no forty metres.
It sails high over the defenders,
and bounces and rolls,
and bounces and rolls,
and stops at the feet
of the opposition striker
who kicks it into the goal.
The winning goal!
The winning goal for the *other* team,
set up by a beautiful forty-metre pass
the *wrong* way, by *Do-wrong Ron*,
legend in his own lunchtime.

Legend in his own lunchtime

Ever since I was five,
when I fell over the ball in our backyard
and landed bad on my arm
(sprained wrist, not broken!),
I've dreamed of scoring the winner.
I've dreamed of handshakes
and slaps-on-the-back
as I walk proudly from the field.
And sure enough,
as I walk off Beechmont Oval,
players slap my back,
shake my hand,
and say, 'Thanks, mate, great kick!'
But they're all players from the *other* team!
My coach comes over, scratching his head,
and says, 'The wrong way, Ron!
Unlucky, lad.'

Dad's in his study, working.
I knock quietly.
He stares at his computer
as I tell him my latest do-wrongism.
He says, 'It's okay, Ron, it'll wear off.'
'It's not foot odour,' I reply.
Dad drifts back into cyberspace.

I can hear Mum humming
in the living room.
She sits cross-legged on the floor,
meditating,
wearing her favourite Indian dress.
Incense stinks out the room.
'Mum, can I talk to you?' I whisper.
'Huuuuuuuummmmmm,' she says.
'It's about something I did today.'
'Huuuuuuuuummmmmmmmmmm.'
Her eyes are closed,
her hands are loose on her knees,
palms facing out.
'Huuuuuuuuummmmmmmmmmmmmmmm.'
'I got ten out of ten in my test, and Ms Fletcher
let me burn down the toilet block to celebrate,' I say.
'Huuuuuuuuuuuuuuummmmmmmmmmmmmmm.'

I give up.
I go to the kitchen,
open the fridge
and reach for the big plastic jug.
Ginger beer cordial.
A huge mouthful, straight from the jug.
'YUUUUKKK.'
*Some*one forgot to add water!
Do-wrong Ron.
Again.

Again

Detention.

Again.

And all I did

when Ms Fletcher asked our class

to name one famous Australian

was put up my hand and offer,

'Mr Connors.'

I chose our Principal

because no one else was saying anything,

and Ms Fletcher gets mad when we don't answer.

It was the first name that came into my head.

Ms Fletcher said, 'Ron. Stand up,

and explain why you've nominated Mr Connors.'

What could I say?

I closed my eyes and pictured Mr Connors...

'Because he's got the best wig in Beechmont!'

All the class giggled.

'Because he loves the sound of his own voice?'

Everyone laughed,

except Ms Fletcher.

'Because he wears a blue tie with a green shirt,

yellow shorts, and long white socks

and my dad says he looks like a pizza

has been thrown over him.'

Sometimes, I just can't help myself.

Help myself

I've tried. I really have.
In my mind I kick the ball in the right direction.
I give correct answers in class.
I mix the cordial in the jug,
but,
between my mind and my feet, hands and mouth,
something gets lost somewhere.
Dad smiles, and says he was like that at my age.
Mum says I should *meditate*.

On Monday, I forgot my homework.
Mum said I should *relax*.
On Wednesday, I poured Coke on my Weet-Bix.
Mum said I should *focus*.
On Friday, I went to the shop for milk
and came home with tuna.
Mum said I should *centre myself*.
Yesterday I hung out the washing, without pegs.
Our clothes floated away on the wind.
Mum said I should *worship the energy source within*.
Dad said I should use pegs,
as we picked underpants from
the flowerbed.

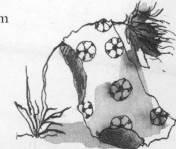

The flowerbed

Maybe one day,
I'll do the right thing at the right time.
Everyone will call me *Do-right Ron*.
I sit in our backyard,
waiting for that special day.
Parrots, rosellas, cockatoos,
squabble over nectar in the bottlebrush.
I sit here, dreaming,
not meditating!

It can't be!
No chance.
In the grass,
a shiver of colour
brown, white, black
and a strange high-pitched sound,
'wee wee wee wee.'
It's a guinea pig,
hiding in the grass.
An escaped
lost
lonely
guinea pig.

He darts under the woodstack by the shed.
Maybe he's hungry?

I kneel down near the wood
holding some carrot.
(I dropped the lettuce
in a bowl of cream,
in my hurry.)
Feeling like a real dork
I try guinea-pig-talk,
'wee wee wee wee.'
Charlie
(that's his name, okay!)
pokes his head out
and nibbles at the carrot.
He's not afraid at all,
or else, he's so hungry
he just has to eat!
My new friend.
My only friend.

My only friend

It makes sense, doesn't it?
I find a pet
that looks like an oversized rat
and squeaks wee wee words when he's hungry!

I've been working all afternoon
on my old cubby house –
with Dad's hammer
and nails
and some spare timber –
to make the cubby escape-proof.
I've covered the floor with grass-clippings,
and cut a hidey-hole in an old shoebox
so Charlie has a place to sleep.

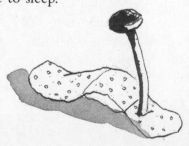

I've hammered my left thumb twice,
cut my middle finger,
and hit my head three times
on the cubby house roof.
Charlie scurries from wall to wall,
kicks up the clippings,
jumps on his shoebox,
and sings 'wee wee wee wee.'
In English, it means
'Mind your head, Ron!
This'll do me!'
Charlie's happy.

Happy

I sit in the cubby
watching Charlie eat a guinea-salad
of carrot, celery, corn and dandelions.

What makes me happy:

Missing class on Thursday afternoons
in summer when the whole school goes
to Beechmont Memorial Pool for sport

*

Going to Chinderah Bay for holidays

*

Remembering the time someone phoned the
school and said there was a bomb in the classroom,
and we were all sent home for the day

*

Sitting in the backyard with Mum listening to my
do-wrong stories ... before she discovered herself

*

Cuddling Charlie up close to my chest and
stroking the soft fur on his back

*

Having a best friend

Best friends

The last week of school before holidays.
Ms Fletcher decides
we should have a Best Friends Ball –
a dance after school on Friday.
The only catch is
the girls have to invite their best friend,
and their best friend must be a boy!
There are fifteen girls and sixteen boys
in the class.
I stare out the window
for the rest of the afternoon
as fifteen girls write invitations,
and fifteen boys write thank-you notes.
Stupid Best Friends Ball!

Best Friends Ball

How embarrassing!
Ms Fletcher wrote an invitation
and sent it to me.
Now I'm sitting under the fig tree
waiting for the Ball to start.
Charlie nestles in close
under my school shirt.

I brought Charlie to school in my bag.
All morning
he munched on his lettuce.
(Yes. I washed off the cream!)
During maths
I could hear a faint
'wee wee wee wee'
coming from the verandah
where my bag was hanging.
In Charlie-speak it meant
'I want carrot!'
or
'Help. I need to go to the toilet!'
Luckily, no one heard or
Charlie might have been
the first guinea pig
expelled from Beechmont Primary.

'As Principal,
I'd like to congratulate
all of class 4–6
on such a groovy idea!
You've got the hall
looking positively... radical!
Yes, that's the word.
Radical.
And hip.
And rocking!
So,
I declare the Best Friends Ball
open,
and I'd like to say...
A RAT!
LOOK OUT. IT'S A RAT!'

a rat?

Charlie scoots across the dance floor.
Ms Fletcher screams.
Simon jumps on Alex's back,
Anna ducks behind Big Pete,
Big Pete hides behind the sound system.
Mr Connors calls out,
'Stay calm! Stay calm!'
He leaps onto a chair.
Class 4-6 spin, bump, twist,
shake and shimmy away
from poor little Charlie.
I only put him down for a minute,
tucked safely in my bag,
but I forgot to close the zip.
Do-wrong!
And now,
madness.
Mr Maddison, the cleaner,
holds a broom
over Charlie's head,
ready to strike.
'Stop!' I shout.
'He's my friend.'

Suddenly, the hall is deathly silent.
I kneel down
holding a piece of Holiday cake.
'Wee wee wee wee,' I whisper.
('Cake, Charlie. Quick!')
Charlie scurries towards me.
Forty pairs of eyes
watch me pick him up,
and put him inside my shirt.
Charlie nibbles at his cake.
I walk to the door,
invisible as a truck.
Mr Connors,
on the microphone,
tells everyone to enjoy themselves
and then says,
'Ron Holman and his pet rat,
see me in five minutes,
in my office.'

Office

I can see the playground
near the back fence
from Mr Connors' office.
A swing, lonely in the breeze,
blows back and forward,
back and forward,
back and forward as
Mr Connors drones on about
'... responsibility to the school
not to let a dangerous,
disease-ridden rodent
cause such havoc.'
I want to tell Mr Connors
that Charlie is a guinea pig,
not a rat,
but now is not the time for a zoology lesson.
'You will spend your holiday, Ron Holman,
writing me an essay on the topic:
Dogs and cats make good pets. Rats do not.'
A cold rain falls on the playground,
and on my holiday.

Holiday

What a way to start a holiday.
Dad's in his study, working.
Mum's at a Meditation, Yoga, Tai-Chi
and Self-Awareness Retreat.
Charlie and I sit in the backyard,
watching a furniture van
reverse into the driveway next door.

New neighbours.
I can see an ancient lady
with grey hair and glasses,
fussing, waving her cane
as if conducting an orchestra,
directing the men as they
unload the furniture.
There's also a girl,
as tall as me,
with long black hair,
and dark eyes.
She's bouncing a ball
and chanting:
'A girl and a ball
and a stupid wall
A girl and a ball
and a boring wall
A girl ... '

 a girl Isabelle

My name is Isabelle.
Yes, I know the joke about
'Isabelle necessary on a bike?'

Can you believe it?
School holidays,
and I'm stuck here
in this pea-size town,
helping Nana Shirl move.
Nana is crazy to want to live here.
She says it might help her.
She hasn't been the same
since Grandpa Bill died.
I liked Grandpa.
He taught me to play golf,
and tennis,
and to kickflip my skateboard,
which is pretty good
for an eighty-five year old.
Him, not me!

I'm eleven.
I miss him.
I'm sure Nana Shirl does too.
All she does now
is sit in her lounge chair,
and doze.

I'd rather be at the beach,
or even at home
with Mum and Dad.
Anywhere but here,
bouncing a ball
against a wall,
waiting for something,
anything,
to happen.

Something, anything, to happen

'Hi.'

'Hi.'

'I'm Ron, this is Charlie.'

'He's cute, for a rat. I'm Isabelle.
You want a game of handball?'

'Sure. He's not a rat though. He's a guinea pig.'

'I know. I was joking. I had one myself.'

'Really. Do you still have him?'

'No. Bishop died of old age,
and from eating too much watermelon.'

'Oh. Sorry.'

'That's okay. It was ages ago.
I made a coffin out of an ice-cream container,
filled it with flowers and grass,
and we buried him
under the cherry tree in our backyard.
I like guinea pigs.'

'Charlie's my best friend.'

My best friend

There's something just right about Isabelle.
I don't normally talk to girls.
Correction.
Girls don't normally talk to me,
but Isabelle is different.
After handball,
we sit in the cubby,
watching Charlie run around.
'He's pretty smart, for a guinea pig,' I say.

Isabelle holds some celery
as Charlie nibbles. She says,
'Most animals are smarter than humans.
They know what they want.
Food, water, a friend,
and somewhere to live.'
'And they don't have to do homework,' I add.
'Or visit relatives during school holidays.'
'Or write thousand-word essays on stupid topics.'

'Maybe Charlie thinks you're *his* pet,
not the other way around.
Ever thought of that?' Isabelle says.
'You bet. That's why I'm good to him.'
Charlie must have heard,
because he jumps straight into my lap
and starts his happy wee wee wee wee.

'What do you think he's saying?' Isabelle asks.
'Give me food! Give it to me now!'
'Not celery again!'
'Why do you humans walk on two legs, not four?'
'What happened to your whiskers, young lady?'
'Get out of my way you clumsy
human, I'm exercising!'
'A shoebox for a home!
Sounds good to me.'

Sounds good to me

'Sounds good to me.'
That's Isabelle's favourite saying.
I ask if she'd like to come over
for dinner,
tonight.
'Sounds good to me,' she says.

So, Isabelle heats the pan,
while I crack the eggs for
my speciality — a potato omelette.
Dad says, 'Breakfast for dinner tonight, Ron?'
But he's in a good mood,
because he can eat in the lounge room,
while Isabelle, Charlie and I sit on the verandah.

Isabelle has two helpings and says,
'You're a good cook, Ron,
better than Nana Shirl.
All she cooks is soup.
Tomato soup.
Vegetable soup.
Beetroot soup.
Onion soup! Yuk!'

'Sloop soup?' I suggest.
'Gloop soup?' says Isabelle.
'Loop soup?'
'Yoop soup?'
We look at each other,
and together we yell,
'POOP SOUP!'

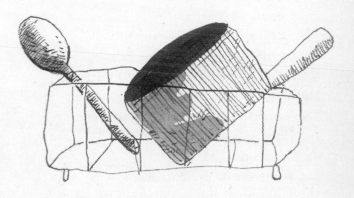

Isabelle Yuk

I like the way Ron does things.
He's different.
Unusual.
Unique.
Who else would crack an egg
with a plastic hammer,
and look so embarrassed
when bits of yolk
shoot off in every direction?

We sit on the verandah, eating.
A magpie lands on the fence, hungry.
Ron cuts a piece of omelette to feed it,
but he flicks it too hard.
The omelette sails right over the fence
and lands, splat,
on Nana Shirl's window,
just as she opens the curtains.
She looks up at the sky, blaming the magpie!

'Sorry, Isabelle,' Ron says quietly.
'You mean, Sorry, Magpie!
Hey, Nana Shirl gave me some money
for ice-creams after dinner.'
'Race you!' I say.
'Last one to the shop
has to eat Poop Soup.'

Ice-creams after dinner

Mr Raducci is singing,
when Isabelle and I cross the finish line
into his shop at Hubert's Corner.
Mr Raducci is a big man.
Legs like tree trunks,
arms like a wood-chopping champion.
Big moustache, big wavy hair,
big glasses hooked over big ears,
and, of course, a *big* voice.
'*Buon giorno*, Ronaldo,' he bellows.
'Do you have a show coming up, Mr R?' I ask.
'*Mama mia*, Ronaldo.
A *musicale*? Me?
No. I sing for myself.'

'Two Cornettos, please,' says Isabelle,
slapping the money on the counter.
'Free ice-creams, *Bella*!
It's a *glorioso* evening. A night for singing.'

And sure enough,
Mr Raducci starts singing
as soon as we leave the store.
His voice is deep and powerful,
like an opera singer.
'La La La La Laaaaaaaaahhhh.
La La La La Laaaaaaaaaahhhh.'
Isabelle and I sit in the bus shelter,
enjoying the performance.
She says, 'Sounds good to me.'
'Sounds *loud* to me!' I reply.

Singing

'Is he always like that?' asks Isabelle.
'No, he can sing even louder!' I say.
'I like him. He reminds me of Grandpa Bill.
Always happy.'
'Happy. And generous,' I add,
crunching on my Cornetto,
as Charlie climbs from inside my shirt
and onto my shoulder.
He can smell ice-cream!
'And the singing – it's enough to crack a window.'
'He wanted to be a singer.
At the Opera House.
He told me he dreamed of travelling the world,
singing.
Then he came here
and fell in love with Beechmont.'
'Fell in love with Beechmont?'

'So he bought this shop,
and now he sings all day.'
'Fell in love with Beechmont?'
'I reckon he should sing for the whole town.'
'Fell in love with Beechmont?'
'It's not that bad, Isabelle.
We've got a creek you can fish in.
On Humpreys Hill
there's a cave full of bats.
In a few weeks there's a carnival
with floats and rides,
and a pie-eating contest
that Mr R always wins.
And Chinderah Bay is only fifty kilometres away.
We go there for most holidays,
except this one.'
'Well I hope the town cheers up my Nana Shirl.'

Cheering Nana Shirl?

I fill a bucket with hot soapy water
and take the ladder, the bucket,
and a sponge next door
and start washing Nana Shirl's window
where the omelette hit.

I should have asked first.
Nana walks into the room,
draws back the curtains,
just as my foot slips
on the wet soapy ladder.
My face squishes against the window,
a flat-faced monster
scaring a frail old lady.
Nana turns ghostly pale,
her mouth open, ready to scream.
'It's me, Nana. Ron.
Ron, the window-cleaner.'
Luckily, Isabelle sees Nana.
I feel double-dorkish,
watching Isabelle calm Nana
as I wipe my red, soapy face.

To make up,
I clean every window of her house.
It takes three hours.
'Good job, Ron.
The sponge works better
than your face,' says Isabelle.
'Is she okay?' I ask.
'Sure. I told her you wanted
to welcome her to Beechmont.
I gave her an aspirin.
She's okay.
She's cooked us some Bloop.'
'Bloop?'
'Broccoli soup!'

Soup

Isabelle and I are sitting
in Nana Shirl's gloomy dining room,
eating cold Bloop.
It's bright and sunny outside,
behind the heavy curtains,
closed windows,
clean glass,
and locked door.
'Say, Nana,
would you like to go for a walk
to the shop with Ron and me?'
'The shop? In this weather?
Too hot. Too bright.
No. No. I'll stay here.
Safe, in the cool.
Safe and sound.'
Nana Shirl shuffles from the dining table,
and slowly sinks into her big blue lounge chair,
removes her glasses,
closes her eyes, and says,
'Go and buy yourself a treat, dear.
You and Ron.
I'll sit here and rest.
Rest, and sleep.
Don't forget to close the door
on your way out.'

On your way out

'Nana won't go out any more,
not since Grandpa died,' Isabelle says,
as we walk to the shop.
'She sits in the lounge room,
sleeping her life away.'
I don't know what to say.
I see a milk carton on the footpath,
so I run towards it,
to show Isabelle my brilliant soccer skills.
I let loose a monster kick.
SPLAT!
Milk shoots out all over my leg and pants.
Milk drips from my hair, from my shirt.
'You look like a ghost. A milk ghost.' Isabelle giggles.
'I thought it was empty.'
At least Isabelle is laughing again.

Laughing again

We take off our shoes
and wade across Sandy Creek.
The water is cold and sparkling
and it tingles.
From the big smooth rock
we dangle our toes
in the running stream.
Charlie slowly walks to the water,
takes a drink,
then scoots back to my side.
'Wee wee wee wee.'
'Delicious,' Isabelle translates.
'I'd like some carrot,
to go with the water,' I suggest.
'Good enough to bottle!'
'Water? I want beer!'
Isabelle scoops up Charlie,
and cuddles him.

'Once I caught a trout,
just around the bend there.
I let him go. I couldn't hurt him.
He had so much colour –
pink and green scales,
like a little darting rainbow.
And once, Dad and I
saw a red-belly black snake
swimming across the creek.
He slithered up onto the far bank.'
Isabelle whips her feet clear of the stream,
splashing water all over me.
'Thanks for washing the milk off!' I laugh.
'Come on, Ron, let's go to the shop.'

The shop

Mr Raducci's shop
is the only one in town.
It's built of timber with old–fashioned signs
painted on the side
that advertise things
you can't buy any more.
Boomerang Tonic
Handy Jack
Bunyip Boot Polish
Mr Raducci refuses to put up new signs.
He says, 'People know what they want.
They don't need to be told.
My signs, they remind me
of when I was a *bambino*.
My papa he sang all night.
And Mama, she played piano.
Songs all day and night.
Not TV.
Not ads telling you
what to eat,
where to shop,
what to wear.
Just *musica*.
Bella musica!'

Bella musica

We can hear Mr R
before we reach the shop.
His voice is like
a slow rumbling earthquake
shaking everything in its path.
We cross the street
and peer through the window.
Mr R is standing with his arms wide,
and legs apart,
his head held high
as the song *bursts* from him.
As he sings, his eyes are closed,
and he's smiling,
as if he's been handed a million dollars,
or he's won an award, for singing!
He tosses his head back
and roars an impossibly deep loud note,
then he bows to his make-believe audience.
He bows left, right, centre,
as we enter, clapping!
We can't help ourselves.
It's such a performance!
I shout, '*More! Encore!*'

More, encore
Isabelle

So far,
in Beechmont,
I've met Ron
who's
different,
unusual,
interesting.
And Mr R
who's
... differenter!
... unusualer!
... interestinger!

It must be something in the water.
Something in the air?

I wonder if it's catching?

Will Isabelle catch it?

Every day this week
Isabelle and I have had lunch
with Charlie in his cubby.
Today Isabelle looks
at my banana and beetroot sandwich,
suspiciously.
'Original choice, Ron.'
'My favourite. Try some?'
Isabelle takes a nervous bite, then smiles.
'Tastes better than it looks,' she says.
'It's my blood-and-guts sandwich!
Delicious.
And it works as lipstick too.'
Isabelle wipes the stain from her lips
as a piece of banana slips from the sandwich.
Charlie zips across and snaffles it.
Isabelle laughs.
'Charlie likes it too!'

'He's a pet with taste,' I say,
and Charlie dives from his shoebox,
straight into his water bowl.
'And style,' says Isabelle.
We both munch on our lunch
as Charlie dog-paddles (pig-paddles?)
around his bowl.
'Charlie should visit Nana Shirl,' I say.
'He'd cheer her up.'

Cheer her up

'It's a rat.
Quick, take it outside!'
Nana Shirl grabs a rolled-up newspaper.
'No, Nana. It's a guinea pig.
He's Ron's pet,' says Isabelle.
'Pet?
That furball is a pet?
Take him away, Ron.
I'm allergic to pets!'
Nana trembles.
'Wee wee wee!'
('Who's she calling a furball!')
'Sorry, Charlie, back to the cubby,' I say.
Isabelle looks sad.
'Give Charlie some extra banana,
for trying, Ron.'
'Okay. See you tomorrow.'

Tomorrow

I'm about to knock
on Nana's back door
when I hear opera
coming from the lounge room.
Nana Shirl is standing
facing the window,
with her eyes closed,
conducting.
She waves her hands
in time with the music,
and as the opera gets louder
she moves her arms faster and higher,
until she almost stumbles with excitement.
She's so involved,
she doesn't see me
standing at the door.

I see her smile, and bow,
as the music stops.
I step back
and fall into the flowerbed.
'Is that you, Isabelle?' Nana calls.
'No, it's me. Ron. I've come to visit.'
And squash your flowers, I say to myself,
as I scramble up.
'Hi, Nana.'

Nana Shirl

Isabelle is right.
Nana Shirl never comes outside.
Never.
Sometimes, when we're
sitting in the cubby
I see Nana watching
through a gap in her curtains
and I wave.
She waves back,
then pulls the curtain closed.
Isabelle says,
'I ask her every day to sit with me
in the backyard,
in the sun,
but she never does.'

I remember seeing Nana
with the music.
She looked happy.

A Charlie moment

Wee wee wee wee
wee wee wee wee wee wee wee
wee wee wee
wee wee wee wee wee
wee wee wee
wee wee wee!
Wee wee weeeeeeee
wee wee wee wee wee
wee.
Wee wee
wee wee wee wee wee wee
wee!
Wee wee wee wee wee wee
wee
wee wee
wee!
Wee wee wee wee wee.
Wee!
Wee wee wee wee!
Wee wee wee
wee wee.

I'm glad I met
the funny kid who feeds me.
I was lost
until I crossed the road
and found his woodstack.
Now I sleep in luxury!
The girl is nice too.
But the old lady scares me.
She tried to hit me
with a paper-sword-thing!
Ron put me in his shirt,
where I feel safe.
But poor Ron doesn't have fur,
just bare skin.
And he doesn't have the right smell...
Too human!

She looked happy

The plan came to me
late at night,
when Charlie and me were
looking out the window
at Isabelle's house.
I'd been thinking about Nana Shirl,
and I remembered how,
whenever I'd done something wrong
at school,
I'd walk home,
shut the door,
draw the curtains,
and sit in my room
with my favourite music
turned up loud –
blotting out the bad feelings.
I'd think of nothing but the song,
and the singer.
If Mum and Dad weren't home,
I'd end up singing
and dancing
around my bedroom
like a madman,
like a popstar.

By the time
they arrived home
and asked me how my day was,
I'd say, Great!
All because of the music.

Music

'Nana Shirl,
you like music, don't you?'
'Music? Not pop music!
Load of noise
as if someone had an accident with a chainsaw!'
'No, Nana. Opera and stuff?'
'Opera is not stuff, Ron.
But yes, I love it.
When I'm listening
I drift away and forget everything.
Why?'

'Oh nothing. I just wondered.
My dad likes music.
He's always playing this old singer
called Bob Dylan
who sounds like he's swallowed his teeth!'
'Young people's music, Ron.
Chainsaw murder.'
'My dad's not young,
but I know what you mean, Nana Shirl.'

Nana sighs, and says,
'My darling Bill and I
would dress in our Sunday-best,
and go to the opera.
We'd sit in the dark,
and hold hands.
The music would wash over us,
and I'd never,
never want to leave.'

A concert

'What do you think, Charlie?
A concert for Nana Shirl,
with Mr R as the star?
He deserves an audience
other than
coffee,
tea,
and toilet paper.
And Nana Shirl needs a welcome party.
Maybe you could do a song as well, Charlie?
A little wee wee wee wee melody?
I wonder if Isabelle can sing.'

Can Isabelle sing?

'Isabelle, are you in the choir at school?'
Isabelle stops rubbing Charlie's back
and looks at me with those dark eyes,
getting darker.
'No way, Ron. Not a chance.
I'm not singing
for Nana Shirl,
you,
Charlie,
Beechmont,
or to save my life! Okay?'
'It was just a thought.'
'Well, you know what *thought* did?
Nothing.
He only thought he did.'
Isabelle and I look at each other,
trying to make sense of what she just said.
We give up.
I say, 'It looks like it has to be Mr R.'

Mr R?

'Say, Mr R, do you sing anywhere?
Apart from the shop?' I ask.
'Some people sing in the shower, Ronaldo.
I *serenata* the bread and milk!'
'Would you like to sing
for a special occasion?'
'What special *occasione*?
The opening of the Olympics?
The Football Grand *Finale*?
The Pope's visit, perhaps?'
'No, Mr R, something important.'
'Oh, something *importante*.
Your rat, Charlie's birthday?'
Charlie fidgets in my shirt.
'No. No. Rats don't have birthdays.
I mean guinea pigs don't have birthdays.
This is *really* important.'

Important

'I thought it would be nice, Mr R,
if the whole town heard you sing.'
'They do, Ronaldo.
I'm always caught by a customer.
This is my Opera House, *amico*.'
'Yes, but you stop when they come in.'
'A true genius is always shy, Ronaldo.'
'Very funny, Mr R.'
'What? You do not think of me as
Raducci the Magnifico?'
'Yes, sure, Mr R.
But why not share your genius?
Your talent deserves a bigger stage.'
'*Scusa?* A bigger stage than behind the counter?
In Beechmont?
Raducci the Magnifico
performs in his shop,
in his Opera House *exclusivo*!

Perhaps Raducci is *Italiano* for shy?
Italiano for humble.
Italiano for...
bashful.'
Mr Raducci carries the milk crate
to the fridge.
'Raducci the Magnifico,
with one twirl of his apron becomes
Raducci the shopkeeper.
Magico!'

Mr R, humming a tune,
loads the milk, slowly,
one carton at a time,
into the fridge.
'Oh well. Bye, Mr R.'
'*Arrivederci*, young Concert Promoter.'

Concert Promoter

Isabelle and I
sit in the bus shelter,
eating Cornettos,
listening to
shy, humble, bashful Mr R,
singing like a tornado.
Isabelle says, 'Why don't we just ask him, Ron?
Would he sing for a sad and lonely old lady?'
'But you heard him, Isabelle.
He won't sing outside his shop!
His Opera House!'
'It's only one old lady!'
'There must be another way to bring music
to Nana Shirl. There has to be.'
Isabelle shrugs.
'Maybe, maybe not.'

Another Charlie moment

Wee wee wee
wee wee
wee wee wee wee wee
wee!
Wee wee wee
wee wee wee wee wee
wee.
Wee wee
wee wee wee wee wee wee
wee!
Wee wee wee wee wee
wee
wee wee
wee!
Wee wee wee wee wee.
Wee!
Wee wee!

Wee wee wee
wee wee!

What is it with this town?
Everyone thinks I'm a rat.
The bloke with boofy hair
at Ron's school.
The old lady.
And now the singer!
All calling me rat.
It's prejudice.
That's what it is!
I'm a guinea pig.
A pure-bred tri-colour shorthair, no less!
My Dad, Harold,
was a show-pig.

Talk about racism.
This is pigism!

Maybe?

Isabelle and I finish our Cornettos
and walk to the top of Humpreys Hill,
and sit in the shade of the Norfolk pine,
planted years ago to honour
all the people from Beechmont
who died in the wars.
We lean against its solid trunk.
'I sang once,
for our school choir.
They put me up the back,
on the end of the row.
When the curtain opened,
I leaned around Big Pete Laird
to see Mum and Dad
and I slipped off the stage.
I grabbed the curtain as I fell...'

Isabelle groans. 'True?'
'Too true.'
'Maybe something like that
happened to Mr R,' she says.
'There are no curtains
in his grocery shop,
so, maybe...'

Charlie dashes round and round
the Norfolk pine.

The Norfolk pine

'When I was six years old,
I climbed this tree.
I wanted to see Chinderah Bay.
It took me hours,
but I made it.
Then, I looked down.
Isabelle, you should never look down!'
'Wee wee wee?'
'Yes, Charlie.
Here's some more lettuce.'
'So, what happened, Ron?'
'I screamed. I shouted.
I cried.
I even threw pinecones
to try to get attention.
After a few hours,
Dad came looking for me.
He got the fire brigade,
and the longest ladder,
and a safety rope.
I came down to a crowd,
all cheering the firemen.'
'Are you scared of heights now?'
'No. I'm scared of fire!'
'Wee wee wee.'
'You're scared of dogs, are you?'
'Wee wee.'

'And cats?'
'Wee wee.'
'And mice?'
'Wee wee wee.'
'And anything with a tail.'
'Maybe Mr R gets stage fright,' says Isabelle.
'Or maybe he's scared of crowds? Or
he doesn't like to dress up
like a popstar,' I say.
'Or maybe he really *is* shy.'
'Wee wee wee wee?'
'No, I don't think he's scared of
swallowing the microphone, Charlie.'

'Wait a minute! That's it!'
'What's it?' asks Isabelle.
'A microphone!'

a microphone

'Simple. Isabelle. Simple.
We can't take Nana Shirl to Mr R,
but we *can* take Mr R to Nana Shirl.'
'But he only sings in his shop!'
'No problem!' I say. 'He doesn't have to leave his shop.
Or even know anyone is listening.'
'Nana Shirl lives five hundred metres away, at least.
No way can she hear Mr R from there.
Nobody is *that* loud.'
'They are with a microphone!
Remember I told you about
Mr Connors shouting *Rat! Rat!*
into the microphone?
He was so loud the building was shaking.'

Shaking Isabelle

Tomato soup for dinner, again.
I watch Nana slowly
dip the spoon into her bowl,
her hand shaking
as she leans forward to eat.
Her lips tremble as she swallows.
'It's good soup, Nana,' I say.
When Nana is finished,
she reaches for her cane
and shuffles across to the sofa,
sits down and closes her eyes.
She's not asleep.
Perhaps she's in a world
where Grandpa Bill lives –
where they're both young.
A world where they're
walking along a beach,
holding hands.
A world where a new town,
cold soup,
and sleeping all day
are a million miles away.
I tidy the dishes,
and think about Ron and his plan.

The plan

Of course,
there's a difference between
having a plan and
making it work.
How do we get a sound system?

The school? Mr Connors?
No chance.
Mr Maddison, the cleaner?
He's a nice old bloke,
even if he did chase Charlie with a broom.

Through my window I see
Isabelle washing the dishes
at Nana Shirl's house.
She looks up,
smiles and waves.
I hold Charlie and wave his front paws.
Isabelle blows Charlie a kiss.
I blush.
She holds up a finger,
as if to say, Wait a minute.
Then she races away,
and comes back with a big sign.

Question: Where was Charlie born?
She turns the sign over.
Answer: New Guinea!

It's the worst joke I've ever heard,
but I still laugh at Isabelle
holding up the sign,
dancing around the kitchen.
Charlie and I wave goodnight.
Tomorrow, I'll ask Isabelle
to come with me and Charlie
to visit Mr Maddison.

Mr Maddison

Mr Maddison lives at the end of Bunbury Street
in a little wooden cottage
with a garden of roses
and camellias
and daisies
and every other flower
that can grow in Beechmont.
It's like stepping into flowerland.
'Hello, Mr Maddison.'
'Hello, young fellow.
Ron, isn't it? How's your rat?'
'Wee wee wee wee!'
('Stop calling me a rat!')
'Fine, Mr Maddison.
He's a guinea pig, actually.
And this is Isabelle.
She's visiting Beechmont
and I thought I'd show her
the best garden in town.'
'Why, thank you, my lad.
Very kind of you to say so.
And what's that you're carrying?'
He points at the garbage bag I'm holding.
'A present, perhaps?
Or has your rat got so very fat
he needs extra feed, indeed?'

'Wee! Wee wee!
Wee wee wee!
Wee wee wee!'
('Fat! Fat rat!
I am a guinea pig!
A sleek and noble guinea pig!')
'No, no, Mr Maddison.
It's a present, I guess.
A bag of compost.
My parents don't garden,
so I thought you'd like our scraps.'
'I would, young man.
Compost is my favourite thing.
Rich, moist and dark.
Some people like chocolate,
some like coffee.
Give me compost any day!'
'Well there's plenty more, Mr Maddison.
I can bring it down here every week, if you want.'
'Sheer heaven, my lad.
I owe you.
Would you like a cup of tea,
or a good old-fashioned lemon barley water?
Made with my own lemons. Come inside.'

Inside

Isabelle and I sit
on the big old couch
as Mr Maddison brings us
two glasses of lemon barley.
He places a bowl of water on the floor,
for Charlie.
'Wee wee wee.'
'That's guinea pig for Thanks, Mr Maddison.'
('No it's not!
I said, It's the least you can do,
after all the insults!')
'It's a great house you've got, Mr Maddison.'
'Full of flowers, Ron. Keeps me busy too.
And smells nice.'
'Do you ever get lonely, Mr Maddison?'
'Never, my lad. Not with the garden,
and then there's cleaning the school,
with you children saying hello every day. Never.'
'It would be awful to be lonely, wouldn't it?'
'Worse than death, young Ron, worse than death.
That's why Beechmont is a good town.
I know everybody here,
and everybody knows me.
Never lonely that way.'

'Isabelle's Grandma has just moved here.

She doesn't know anyone yet.

So Isabelle and I have come up with a plan.'

Mr Maddison looks worried.

'You're not trying to marry me off, are you, Ron?'

'No, Mr Maddison. It's a simple plan.

But . . . we need help.

We need something that's not ours.'

'Money, perhaps?'

'No, no, no, Mr Maddison.

You know how Mr Raducci is a fabulous singer?

And how he only sings in his shop?

Well, Nana Shirl loves music,

but she never leaves her house.'

'I see. So how do you get Mr R to sing for Nana Shirl?'

'We make him loud. *Very* loud.'

Mr Maddison leans back in his chair,

takes a long drink of lemon barley water,

rubs his hair, and says,

'I see. Well, give me a few days, young man,

and I'm sure I can arrange something.

Another drink?'

'Thanks.'

Thanks

On our way home
we walk past the school.
I show Isabelle my classroom,
and the new climbing equipment
all our parents built last Easter.
We climb to the top of the crossbars
and sit with our legs swinging.
Isabelle tells me about her school
in the city,
with twenty classrooms
and more children
than all the population of Beechmont.
I stare across the paddock
behind the school
and try to picture so many classrooms,
so many teachers,
so many children
calling me *Do-wrong Ron.*
I'm glad I live in Beechmont.

Beechmont

Isabelle

Beechmont isn't so bad, I guess.
I like Ron,
and Charlie.
Yesterday, we visited this old guy
who lives in a house full of flowers.
He gave us the sweetest cordial
I've ever tasted.
As we left, he cut some roses,
and daisies,
and tied them with a ribbon.
He gave them to me –

'For your Nana.
But don't tell her I sent them, okay?
Tell her you picked them.
To cheer her up.
To welcome her to our small town.'

Wee wee wee

wee wee - wee wee wee

wee wee - wee.

wee wee - wee wee wee.

wee wee wee wee wee

Wee wee wee wee wee

wee wee wee.

Wee wee wee

wee wee wee wee wee

wee.

Wee wee

wee wee wee wee

wee wee

wee!

Wee wee

wee wee wee

wee

wee wee.

I like fruit.
Apples, oranges — peeled, thank you.
Carrot — yum.
Lettuce — delicious, even with cream.
But, I hate flowers!

Yesterday
at the flower-man's house,
I sneezed all day.
My eyes watered.
My ears itched.
And I remembered how
when I was a guinea piglet
I went to smell a rose,
and got stung on the nose
by a bee!
I ran around in circles,
squealing,
and crying,
until Harold came
and pulled the bee-sting out
with his long teeth.
He spat it at the rose.
I hate flowers!

Small town

It only took Mr Maddison
three days to ring me.
'The sound system is yours, Ron.
Just keep that compost coming, okay?'
'Sure, Mr Maddison. And thanks!'
I put the phone down,
thinking of music,
and Nana Shirl,
smiling,
laughing,
feeling happy to be in Beechmont.

Music

Ron has a musical plan,
so I play a CD of opera
for Nana Shirl.
Lots of violins and cellos,
with a really booming drum,
like a caged animal trying to escape.
I watch Nana, listening,
her eyes closed,
her fingers tapping,
as if she's in a trance.
I stretch out on the sofa,
close my eyes,
and let the music take me.

Where does it take me?
To sleep, that's where!
I wake up to Ron tapping on the window,
smiling at me,
sleeping like an old lady.
I look at Nana Shirl.
She's sleeping and the music has stopped.
I hope I didn't dribble in my sleep,
like Nana does.
I don't fancy Ron seeing me as a dribbler!
I wave him round to the back door.
It's time to start planning for Nana's concert.

Isabelle

Nana's concert

Ron and I have an action plan.
Monday morning.
When everything in town is quiet.
Ron will handle the sound
from Mr R's shop,
and I'll get Nana Shirl
to stroll around the garden
and admire the flowers.
It'll work.
I'm sure it will.
It has to.
As Mr Maddison says:
to be lonely would be worse than death.
It *has* to work.

It has to work

Stupid sound system!
Charlie and me are outside Mr R's shop,
hiding in the bushes.
Dad's extension cord trails
into the toilet block power-point
behind the shop.
But I can't get this stupid thing to work!
It's nine o'clock.
Mr R is inside,
serving customers,
and yes,
he's been singing all morning!
'Come on, Charlie, what's wrong with this machine?'
Charlie scurries down the path to the toilet block.
It's a pretty smart animal
that knows where to go when he needs to.
I flick the switch on and off, hoping it'll start.
Nothing.

I hear Charlie calling
'wee wee wee wee'
from the toilet.
'Not now, Charlie,' I whisper.
'Wee wee wee wee.'
'Yes, Charlie, that's what a toilet is for.'
'Wee wee wee wee.'
'SSSSHHHHHHHHHHH.'
'Wee wee wee wee!'
'Okay, Charlie, you win, I'm coming.'
I run to the toilet block, pick Charlie up,
and tuck him inside my shirt.
Then I notice the power-point isn't switched on.
Do-wrong Ron has struck again.

Even a guinea pig knows more than me.
'Thanks, Charlie.'
I try the sound–system once more.
Still nothing.
'What now, Charlie?'
'Wee wee.'
'Smack it? Good idea, Charlie.'
One sharp blow.
'OUCH!'
Do-wrong Ron, again.
'Wait! Charlie, look,
the light is on.
It's working!'
Okay, okay, okay.
Now the microphone and lead.
It has to ...
reach the ...
open window ...
It does, just.
Two minutes to concert time.
Who's that coming around the corner?
'Hide, Charlie. Hide.'

'Oh, hi, Mr Connors.'

Mr Connors

'Hello, Ron. How's your holiday?'
'Fine, sir. I've started on the essay, sir.'
'Still have your rat I see.'
'His name's Charlie, sir. He's a guinea pig.'
'Rat. Mouse.
Guinea pig. Whatever.'
'Wee. Wee.
Wee. Wee.'
('Human. Monkey.
Gorilla. Whatever.')
Mr Connors stammers,
'Say, isn't that...?
What is that black box?
It looks like...
here...
let me have a closer look.'
'I can explain, sir. I can.
But not now.
Trust me, sir.'
'Trust someone with a pet rat?
Rubbish!
What are you doing with school property
there in the bushes?
What on earth...?'
'This, sir. Listen.'

Listen

I flick the switch.
Silence.
Then Mr Raducci's voice **booms**
from the speakers
carefully positioned on the bus shelter roof,
aimed up the hill towards Nana Shirl's.
'Bella Rosa, bella Rosa...'
I can see Mr R at the counter,
his arms outstretched,
his head tilted back,
a smile in his eyes,
his right foot tapping along.
His shoulders lift
as he reaches the end
and lets loose one mighty burst
of sound that even Nana Shirl can hear,
I'm sure.
Nana Shirl...

Mr Connors is standing,
open-mouthed,
staring at the bus shelter,
looking confused,
and a little scared,
as if the shelter has grown a voice.
Our eyes meet,
then I turn and run,
as fast as I can
up the hill to Nana Shirl's,
to see if she's with Isabelle,
listening,
in the garden.

Isabelle
In the garden

It's taking forever
to convince Nana Shirl
to come outside.
I hope Ron is running late
or it'll be all over
by the time we make it to the door.

'Nana. Yesterday I saw a mouse
nibbling on the spinach.'
'Not the spinach!
It's ready for eating.
Dirty mouse!
Be a dear, Isabelle.
Run outside and pick what's left.
You've worked so hard
in the garden for me.
There's a good girl.'
'Wouldn't you like to come
with me, Nana?' I plead.
'No, no, run along, dear.
I don't want that mouse to eat it all.'

I step outside.
I can hear Mr R's voice
trumpeting up the hill.
'Funiculi, funicula!'
Nana's favourite.

And here's Ron, running,
as though he's being chased.
Oops…

Oops...

'Stupid garden hose!'
'Ron, are you okay?'
'No. My wrist.
It hurts like crazy.'
'Nana! Quick!'

Isabelle

Nana, quick?

Nana Shirl comes to the window,
sees Ron rolling on the grass,
holding his wrist.
She closes the curtain.
'Nana!' I call again.
She walks to the back verandah,
stops for a second,
then holds the railing
as she inches down the stairs
into the garden.
She's carrying a bandage
and a long wooden spoon.
Nana hobbles towards Ron,
kneels down,
and places the spoon
along Ron's wrist.
She wraps the bandage tightly
around both the spoon and the wrist.
'To keep it straight,' she says.
Ron isn't crying
but I hold his (good) hand anyway.

We look at each other
as Mr R's song finishes,
and a man in a suit
comes puffing into the backyard,
calling, 'Ron Holman.'
Ron answers, 'Here, Mr Connors.'
And I know now
that our brilliant, glorious, original plan is over.

As we all help Ron inside,
a thunderous voice comes
echoing across town.
'Sliced wholemeal,
fat-free milk,
and your favourite Iced Vo-Vos, Mrs Parsons.
That'll be $8.25, *grazie*.
So how's life been treating you?'

A (sad)
Charlie moment

Wee wee wee

wee wee

wee wee wee wee wee

wee.

Wee wee wee

wee wee wee wee wee

wee.

Wee wee

wee wee wee wee wee wee

wee.

Wee wee!

Wee wee wee

wee wee wee wee wee

wee.

Wee wee.

My friend Ron sobbed,
last night, in his sleep.
I wriggled on his bed.
He waved his
stiff white arm,
and he cried,
'No. Charlie.
Look out!'
I snuggled in close
to his chest
and whispered good things.
I love my furless friend.

So how's life been treating you?

I'm sitting at my desk
with my right arm in plaster
and my left hand holding a pen
trying to write an essay.
My second essay this holiday.
The topic:
Using school property in the correct manner.
How am I supposed to come up
with a thousand words on that?
Mr Maddison is probably sitting at home
writing the same thing.
He only tried to help.
He knew Mr Connors
wouldn't loan the sound system,
so he just borrowed it for the day
to make Nana Shirl happy.

I haven't seen Mr R since Monday.
A 'Closed' sign hangs on his door.
Mr R never closes his shop,
except at Christmas,
and on Beechmont Carnival Day.
At least Isabelle didn't get into trouble.

She told Nana Shirl the whole story –
our plan, the sound system,
Mr Maddison and the compost,
Mr R's amazing voice,
everything.
She said Nana Shirl had a cry
and then told her to visit me
while she made some personal phone calls –
probably to tell Isabelle's parents to pick her up
and take her home,
away from people like me.

At least I've still got Charlie.
When I fell over,
I was so scared of squashing Charlie,
nestled inside my shirt,
that I put my arm out to cushion my landing
and that's how my wrist broke.
That's why I'm sitting here,
writing an essay,
and trying hard
not to think about Mr R.

Thinking about Mr R.

Maybe
he's left town forever.
Because of me
and my stupid plan.
'Wee wee wee wee.'
'Thanks, Charlie.
I'm glad *you* thought
it was a good idea.
Can you find Mr R for me?'
'Wee wee wee wee wee!'
'Yes, I know you're a guinea pig,
not a bloodhound!
But what if he never comes back?'
'Wee wee wee!'

'Yes, I'm sure we'll find somewhere
to buy your carrots!'
'Wee wee wee wee wee?'
'Do I want to hear
an old guinea pig saying?
Sure, why not?'
'Wee wee wee.
Wee wee wee wee.'
'*A Monday lasts for hours.*

But a Saturday lasts forever.
I don't know what it means,
but thanks, Charlie.
Do you know tomorrow is Saturday,
and Beechmont Carnival Day?'
'Wee wee?'
'Yes, of course you can come, Charlie.'

Saturday

Beechmont Carnival Day.
Dad says I can go with Isabelle.
He isn't mad at me.
'It's the thought that counts, Ron.'
That was all he said.
Mum phones from the Retreat.
She wants to come home early
to look after me,
but I tell her I'm fine.

I tell her I'm meditating
to help ease the pain in my arm.
She shows me how to go
'Huuuuuuuuummmmmm'
over the phone.

Isabelle waves from her gate.
I cup Charlie in my good hand,
and off we go.
'Wee wee wee, wee wee?'
'Yes, Charlie,
I'll buy you a showbag.'
'Wee wee wee?'
'Yes, there are lots of rides.'
'Wee?'
'And games.'
'Wee?'
'Yes, Charlie,
I'll buy you some fairy-floss, okay!'

Beechmont Carnival

'Hi, Isabelle.'
'Hi, Ron. How's your wrist?'
'Still broken.'
We head for Beechmont Park.
It's the only day when everyone in town
comes together,
apart from Anzac Day, of course.
I see a young boy in a stroller
near the farm animals.
'Donkey, donkey,' he says,
as he pats a goat.

Isabelle and I hop on the ferris wheel.
The old wheel starts with a clank of metal
and slowly lifts us high above the park,
above the jumping castle
and the food stalls.
I can smell the sausage sizzle
and the onions.
We go way above the stage
where Mr Connors is giving a long-winded speech.

We're so high
I can see Hubert's Corner
and Mr R's shop.
Closed.
Last year he won the pie-eating contest
for a record fifth time.
I can see my house
and Nana Shirl's.
She said No thanks
when we asked
if she wanted to come with us.
Not even a carnival will get her outside.
Only me breaking my wrist.

We're as high as the wheel can go.
If we look really hard,
we can see Chinderah Bay
in the blue distance.

The blue distance

The ferris wheel creaks to a stop
with Isabelle, Charlie and me
higher than anyone.
So high that even Mr Connors is small,
and his words are faint.
But I'm sure I can just hear,
'Ron Holman'.
Oh no, I'm in trouble again.
Am I going to be blamed
for stopping the ferris wheel?
Everyone at the carnival is looking up at us,
and Mr Connors points
and says something I can't make out.
A soft cheer,
and the sound of clapping
reaches Isabelle and me on the breeze.
We look way down to the stage
where Mr Connors is shaking hands
with someone.
It looks like...
It is...

Mr Raducci!
He's back!
I knew he wouldn't miss the pie-eating contest.
He's probably won again,
for the sixth year in a row,
and Mr Connors
is going to give him an award.
Maybe a golden-pie trophy?

But instead of a speech,
Mr R looks up at me,
and Isabelle,
bows,
waves,
and starts
SINGING!
In public!
Nana Shirl's favourite opera.
And maybe,
just maybe,
if she has a window open,
she'll hear him.
But Nana's house
has all the windows closed,
and the curtains drawn.

Singing

We lean over to listen.
I hold Charlie in both hands
in case he gets nervous.
Are guinea pigs scared of heights?
'Wee wee wee wee.'
'Yes, Charlie, it is a great view.'
Mr R is not alone onstage.
He has the school choir,
singing in four-part harmony.
And the sound rises up.
It's so beautiful.
Mr R even dances a little.
Then he sings a perfect
deep bass note
that's so strong
it rocks the ferris wheel –
although it may be the breeze –
and he ends with a loud
swelling 'Laaaaaahhhhhh.'
I grip Isabelle's hand
and squeeze.

She smiles,
and points to somebody on stage
and I'm sure,
yes!
It's Nana Shirl!
Nana Shirl is the conductor!
The crowd applauds.
Then they raise their hands,
and look up at us and cheer.

Cheer

On stage
Mr Connors presents Nana Shirl
with a glorious bouquet of flowers.
'To the newest citizen of Beechmont.
Welcome.'
Nana accepts the flowers,
bows to the audience,
then turns to the ferris wheel
and waves.
'Wee wee wee wee.'
'Nana Shirl does look happy, Charlie.'
'Wee wee wee wee.'
'No. She's been given flowers, not fairy-floss.'
'Wee wee wee wee.'
'We know you hate flowers, Charlie.'
'Wee wee wee!'
'Yes, Charlie, you love fairy-floss!'
Mr Maddison helps Nana offstage.
The ferris wheel clunks into gear,
and slowly brings us
back down to the carnival.

The Carnival

Everyone gathers at the ferris wheel.
Mr Connors pushes through,
followed by Nana Shirl and Dad.
'Mr Connors. I've almost finished the essay, sir.'
'Forget the essay, Ron,' he says.
He turns to the crowd.
'Parents, students,
townsfolk of Beechmont.
I take great pride
in presenting Ron Holman with...
The Beechmont Carnival
Community Spirit Award.
Well done, Ron.'
Mr Connors shakes my hand
and presents me with a shining medal
in a beautiful wooden box.
Isabelle says, 'Sounds good to me, Ron.'
Dad steps forward and gives me a big hug.
'That's my boy, Ron.'

I don't think I can take much more
without knowing why
everyone is smiling at me.
Nana Shirl takes my hand
and whispers in my ear,
'I had to make a few phone calls, Ron,
to let everyone know what you
and young Isabelle did
to try to make a sad old lady
feel welcome in Beechmont.
Thank you, Ron.
Thank you.'

Thank you

Isabelle and I help Nana Shirl
stroll around the carnival.
She buys some blackberry jam,
and pumpkin scones,
and homemade soup.
More soup!
'I'm sure it's not as good as mine,' says Nana.
Isabelle is about to answer,
but I quickly say,
'No one makes soup like you, Nana!'
'Why, thank you, Ron.'
Isabelle pulls a face, and Nana sees her.
'I'm glad *someone* appreciates my soup, Ron.'
'Do you want to hear a joke, Nana?' I ask.
'Is it smutty? Or rude?'
'No, Nana.'
'Oh well, pity.' Nana grins.

'Where was Charlie born?' I ask.
Nana leans on her cane,
eyes closed,
straining for an answer,
and says,
'Charleville!'
'No.'
'Charlestown!'
'No.'
'Charlton?'
'No.'

Nana Shirl smiles slowly
at Isabelle and me,
and answers,
'New Guinea!'
'You've got it, Nana!'

You've got it, Nana

Isabelle and I walk home with Nana Shirl.
'That's enough noise and excitement
for one day,' she says.
'But you liked Mr R's singing,
didn't you, Nana?' asks Isabelle.
Nana looks at me, and winks.
'I did indeed, Isabelle. Beautiful.
Not like a chainsaw at all.'
'He might sing in his shop for you, Nana.
If you visit him,' I say.
'One day at a time, Ron.'
'Wee wee wee wee,' Charlie butts in.
'Would you like Charlie to stay with you?' I ask,
taking him out of my shirt.
Nana holds up her hand, quickly, as though
Charlie may jump on her at any moment.
What is it with adults and guinea pigs?
'No, thank you, Ron,' says Nana.
'You and Isabelle, and Charlie,
go back to the carnival.
I'm going to sit and rest.
And maybe listen to some music.
Enjoy the day.'

Enjoy the day

What a day!
A *Do-right Ron* day!
I did something right, at last.
Isabelle and I go on every ride, twice.
Charlie enjoys all the spinning,
twisting, and rolling.
He nibbles the fairy-floss.
'Wee wee wee.'
'Better than carrot?'
We see Mr Maddison,
walking by the cattle
at the animal enclosure.
I start to apologise, but he laughs
and says, 'Ron, it was a good thing you did.
And I didn't get into trouble at all.
So don't worry, my lad.
In fact, Mr Connors used his influence
so I could come here today
to collect all the fertiliser I need
for my garden.

Nothing like manure for flowers, Ron.
Manure, and compost, of course.
A special treat.'

Mr Raducci is sitting
at a table
with a long line of people
waiting for him to sign
their carnival programmes.
He sees me,
waves,
stands,
takes off his hat,
and bows.
Mr R the popstar!

a special day

'Mr Raducci, I'm sorry about...'
'Sorry?
Sorry!
Raducci the *Magnifico*
is proud of you, Ronaldo.
Proud!
You, and Bella.
Now the world is my stage, my *scena*.'
'You're not leaving us, are you, Mr R?'
'Never, Ronaldo.
But I shall sing
in the *strada*,
in the *piazza*,
at your *scuola*,
in *chiesa*.
Raducci the *Magnifico*
has found an audience, Ronaldo.
Because of you.
You and Bella.'

Bella

Mr R reaches under the table,
and gives Isabelle
a cardboard box
tied with a bright red ribbon.
He says,
'For Bella.
I bought it between rehearsals.
A present for Bella.
Open it together,
on the ferris wheel.'
He winks,
then goes back to signing autographs.

A Charlie moment,
on Beechmont

Wee wee wee wee wee

wee.

Wee wee wee

wee wee wee wee wee

wee.

Wee wee

wee wee wee wee wee wee

wee.

Wee wee!

Wee wee wee

wee wee wee wee wee

wee.

Wee wee.

Wee wee

wee wee wee wee wee wee

wee.

Wee wee!

Wee wee

wee wee wee wee wee wee

wee.

Wee wee!

What a strange town.
Last week I was called a rat.
A fat rat!
Today, I'm Charlie
or
Sweet little guinea pig.
Everyone wants to pat me,
even the flower-man
who carries cow poo
around in a bag.
Mr Maddison,
that's his name.

I like the cup-and-saucer ride,
and the up-and-down roller coaster,
but I like the big spinning wheel the
best.
I hope we go on that again.
You can see forever.
It's like flying.
Charlie –
No
Super-Charlie –
the flying guinea pig!

The Ferris wheel

We have a ticket for one more ride.
The box sits, unopened,
between us.
With a lurch and a clank,
we're lifted high above Beechmont.
I hold Charlie on my knee.
We can see my school,
and Sandy Creek,
and the Norfolk pine
standing straight and tall on Humpreys Hill.
At the highest point,
Isabelle places the box on her lap.
She smiles.
'I bet it's a tape of Mr R,
for Nana.'
'No, I reckon it's a box of chocolates,
from his shop.'
'Wee wee wee?'
'Yes, Charlie,
it might be fairy-floss.
And yes, you can have some more!'
Isabelle lifts the lid.
Sitting inside is a
brown-and-white guinea pig!

The card reads:
Her name is Ruby!
'Charlie, meet Ruby.
Ruby, meet Charlie.'
'Wee wee wee wee.'
'Wee wee wee.'
'Charlie says, Hello.'
'Ruby says, Are we flying?'
'Of course guinea pigs can fly.'
'And swim.'
'And most definitely, eat!'

We sit in the perfect sunshine,
high above the town.
Isabelle looks at Charlie and me,
down at the carnival,
across at Mr R's shop,
and up the hill to Nana Shirl's house.
Then she says,
'Ruby might grow to love Beechmont.'
'Sounds good to me,' I say.
'Wee wee wee wee.'
'Wee wee wee wee.'
Ruby and Charlie obviously agree.

A (final) Charlie moment

Wee wee

wee wee wee

wee wee wee

wee.

Wee wee!

Wee wee

wee wee wee wee wee

wee.

Wee wee!

Wee wee

wee wee wee wee

wee wee

wee.

Wee wee!

Wee wee

wee wee wee wee wee wee

wee.

Wee wee!

I asked Ron
to be my best human,
for the wedding.
In my guinea house.
Me and Ruby – married.
We had our honeymoon
in the water bowl.
Swimming.
Soaking up the sun.

Ron and Isabelle,
and the old lady, Shirl,
have just left.
They've gone to the shop
for an ice-cream.
They were singing.

Steven Herrick was born in Brisbane,
the youngest of seven children. At school his favourite subject
was soccer, and he dreamed of football glory while he worked
at various jobs, including fruit picking. Now Steven writes for
children and teenagers and visits many schools each year. He
loves talking to the students and their teachers about poetry,
and soccer. He likes the main character in *Do-wrong Ron*
because Ron is good-hearted and always tries to do the right
thing, and Steven wonders if the 'wrong' thing is really wrong,
or if it's just how people take it.

Steven's books for young adults include: *Love, Ghosts and
Nose Hair* (shortlisted in the 1997 Children's Book Council
awards and the NSW Premier's Literary awards), *A Place Like
This* (shortlisted in the 1999 CBC awards, the NSW Premier's
Literary awards, and commended in the 1998 Victorian
Premier's Literary Award), and *The Simple Gift* (shortlisted
in the 2001 CBC awards and the NSW Premier's Literary
awards). His books for children include:
My Life, My Love, My Lasagne, The Spangled Drongo
(Winner in the 2000 NSW Premier's Literary awards),
Love Poems and Leg-Spinners, and *Tom Jones Saves the World*.

Steven lives in the Blue Mountains
with his wife and two sons.